# 200

# Brilliant Golf Facts

## For Golf Fans

All Facts are correct as of
April 7th 2022

The golf term "caddie" comes from the French word Cadet.

It would take 4 miles of walking to reach all 18 holes of a regulated golf course.

Golf balls used to be handmade. These golf balls were made of leather stitched into a spherical shape that contained feather stuffing from geese or chickens.

Only 20% of all the golfers in the world have achieved a handicap of less than 18.

Although modern golf traces back to 15th-century Scotland, the sport's ancient roots are heavily debated between different ancient civilizations.

One theory suggests that golf came from the Roman stick-and-ball game, paganica. Others point to the Chinese chuiwan played between 8th and 14th century China.

A golf ball is more likely to travel further during the summer rather than during the winter.

Generally speaking, a golfer has a 1 in 12,500 chance of scoring a hole in one during a game. In the United States, you have a 1 in 4,292 chance of getting run over by a car.

The average professional
golf club has a lifespan
of three years.

Celine Dion owns a golf
course in Quebec.

The 2010 record of most holes played in the
year belongs to Richard Lewis. He played
over 600 rounds within the calendar year.

Roughly 22.8% of golfers are
female.

The Augusta National Golf Club is the most famous golf club in the world.

A golf ball has between 300 to 500 dimples on its surface.

Over 125 thousand golf balls are hit into the water at the 17th hole of Sawgrass's Stadium Course.

On average, 300 million golf balls are lost in the U.S. per year.

The world's longest golf hole is the 7th hole of the Sano Course at the Satsuki Golf Club in the country of Japan measured at 964 yards.

Kassandra Komma got the surprise of her life when she made the first hole in one in her career and then hit another hole in one in the same round.

The Tactu Golf Club in Peru stands as the highest golf course in the world. Found in the mountains of Morococha, Peru, the Tactu Golf Club's lowest point towers 14,335 ft over sea level.

Babe Zaharias was the first woman to make it to the PGA Tour event in 1945.

The Solheim Cup is the biggest competition in women's professional golf. The Lake Hefner Course in Oklahoma 1961, Lou Kretlow achieved this record on the 16th hole.

The golfer Seve Ballesteros has won over 90 international competitions including five major championship victories.

Nick Faldo has won the United States master a total of three times and ranked first in the world for 97 weeks in a row.

Tiger Woods and Sam Snead are tied for the most PGA Tour victories with 82 wins.

Most golf clubs break due to poor swings.

The average golf tee is made from plastic or a variation of hardwood.

Modern-day golf clubs commonly use a mixture of stainless steel and titanium to make the body.

France once established a naked golf course. The La Jenny Naturist Golf Course is located on the west coastline of France.

The average professional
golf club has a lifespan
of three years In.

In 2016 golf returned into
the Olympic games after
112 years.

The term golf originated from the
Netherlands. The Dutch word for club is
"kolve" or "kolf".

The oldest known golf course in
the world is The Old Course at
St. Andrews in Fife, Scotland.

Golf may be an elite sport now but it was originally simply a game that shepherds played to pass the time.

To meet regulation standards, golf holes must have a diameter of 4.25 inches and a depth of 4 inches.

Golf holes do not stay in one place and are moved regularly.

At one point in its history, golf was banned in Scotland, In 1457. Scotland was at war and needed to focus on military training.

Mary Queen of Scots brought the game to the French during her stay in the country in the 15th century and was believed to be the first female player ever.

The first handicap system was invented by a female player named Issette Pearson in 1893.

On average it takes 5 and a half hours to complete an 18 hole golf course.

A dentist named Dr. George Grant is credited with designing the golf tee. He patented it in 1899.

Before the golf tee was designed, golfers used to build a small mound of sand or soil to place the ball.

The oldest continuously running golf club in the U.S. is The Dorset Field Club. It was founded in 1886 when Arvin Harrington.

The Americans are credited for coining the term "birdie". A player, Ab Smith, hit a good shot and called it a "bird of a shot".

"Fore!" is a golfer's way to warn other players about an errant ball. This is a warning to help prevent any injuries. It is the shortened version of afore or before, which was an old Scottish warning that means "look out ahead".

The lowest golf score listed on the Guinness World Records belongs to Rhein Gibson of Australia. He recorded 2 eagles and 12 birdies on a par 71.

The longest drive ever recorded was made by Michael Hoke Austin, an English-American pro golfer. He drove 515 yards during the 1974 U.S. National Seniors Tournament.

The most expensive club ever sold ($181,000) is also the oldest verified club.

The first rule of etiquette among players is the safety of other golfers.

Golf is often referred to as the gentlemen's game.

Before 1939, golfers carried as many as 30 clubs to accommodate different shots in a game.

A tour player's odds of hitting a hole in one is 3000-1.

Other than the javelin throw, golf is the only sport ever to be played by a human on the moon. Using a six-iron, Alan Shepard, Jr. drove a ball using a one-handed swing on Feb. 6, 1967.

Tiger Woods has received the player of the year award 10 times.

---

Doug Ford predicted his Masters victory and exact score of 283 in 1957.

---

Phil Mickelson Is Right-Handed but plays with his Left due to mirroring his father's stance at a young age.

---

The longest putt verified by the Guinness Book of World Records is 395 feet.

# Tiger Woods Made His First Hole-in-One at Eight Years Old.

The rarest score of all (the condor) is when a golfer makes a hole in one on a par 5. This score is so unique, it has only been recorded 4 times.

# Las Vegas's Shadow Creek golf course is the most expensive course to play at $500 for 18 holes.

# Golf Was Invented in Scotland.

The biggest golfing green is 28,000 square feet at the International Golf Club in Massachusetts.

---

The average drive speed of a LPGA women's player is 96 mph.

---

The average drive speed of a PGA Men's Player is 150 mph.

---

If you choose to walk for 18 holes, you will walk roughly 4 miles and burn around 2,000 calories.

There are 34,011 golf courses in the world.

Jack Nicklaus holds the most major championships at 18 with Tiger Woods in second with 15.

Brandon Grace shot a 62 in the third round at Royal Birkdale Golf Course in 2017 for the lowest round at a major.

Both Chip Beck (1991) and Adam Hadwin (2017) had 13 birdies in a round.

Andrew Magee made a "hole in one" on a par 4 in 2001 at TPC Scottsdale. The hole was 332 yards long.

Tiger Woods holds the title for lowest scoring average at major championships over his career.

# Harry Vardon won the British open 6 times.

Nick Faldo scored 25 Ryder cup points in his career.

Sergio Garcia won his 1st PGA golf tournament aged 21.

---

3 shots under par on a hole is called an Albatross or Double Eagle.

---

Scott Base Golf Club in Antarctica is the most southerly golf club in the world.

---

PGA Tour professionals pay their own travel expenses (top golfers are covered by sponsors).

The average golf course on the PGA Tour is roughly 7,000 yards in length.

A par 5 typically ranges from 460-600 yards.

A par 4 typically ranges from 230-460 yards.

A par 3 typically ranges from 90-230 yards.

USA is the country with the most golf courses in the world.

The country with the most golf courses per capita is Scotland.

Golf courses are present in 85% of countries worldwide.

Over 456 million rounds of golf are played annually.

The golf industry is worth approximately $70bn annually.

Every year several billion is raised for charity through golf.

A putter typically makes up around 41% of shots during a golf round for proffesionals.

The sand wedge was invented by professional golfer Gene Sarazen.

The PGA Tour first started in 1929.

Charles Kocsis was the youngest ever winner on the PGA Tour in 1931 at 18 years, 6 months and 9 days.

Tiger Woods has spent the most weeks as golf's world number 1 with 281 weeks.

An average of 3.6 million people tune into PGA Tour coverage at any time during a tournament.

245 Golfers make up the PGA Tour.

---

The lowest ever tournament score in relation to par on the PGA Tour was −33 by Steve Stricker in the 2009 Bob Hope classic.

---

The four majors in the professional golf calendar are The Masters, The US Open, The USPGA & The Open.

---

When asked, 81 PGA Tour players voted Augusta National as their favourite course to play followed by Harbour Town.

There has been one hole in one on a par 4 on the PGA Tour by Andrew Magee in 2001.

---

The term 'Green' in golf only refers to the area of the golf course and not the colour.

---

Two golfers made an appearance in the 1996 golf film, Happy Gilmore. Mark Lye & Lee Trevino.

---

Byron Nelson is responsible for the most famous winning streak in golf history. In August 1945, Byron Nelson won the Canadian Open by four strokes. This was his 11th consecutive victory on the PGA Tour and he won 18 of the 30 tournaments he played in 1945.

Samuel L. Jackson is an avid golfer. In fact, the star of flicks like "Pulp Fiction" and "Django Unchained," has a contract clause to play golf twice a week whenever he films movies.

---

The very first nationally-televised golf tournament, the 1953 World Championship of Golf, featured an incredible finish from Lew Worsham.

---

Alice Miller presently holds the LPGA Tour's record for fastest round, completing 18 holes in one hour, 26 minutes, and 44 seconds.

---

Northern Canadian territory Nunavut's annual Toonik Tyme Festival includes a nine-hole golf tournament. With temperatures well below freezing, golfers play on a sheet of ice, using fluorescent balls, in fear of losing them in the snow.

Phil Mickelson's stayed 26-years inside the world's top 50.

Lydia Ko's had 10 LPGA Tour victories before turning 19.

In 1975, 5 year old Cosby Orr shot a hole in one to set a record.

Augusta National co-founders Bobby Jones and Clifford Roberts acquired the original 365-acre property for $70,000. In 2017, $71,500 was the payout for 31st place in the event.

It's been 30 years since someone has aced the par-3 12 hole. That someone was Curtis Strange, with a 7-iron, in 1988.

---

The first Masters playoff, in 1935, was a single-day, 36-hole competition. Gene Sarazen beat Craig Wood, 144 to 149.

---

Tom Weiskopf shares the record for worst single-hole score in the Masters, thanks to the 13 he took on the 12th hole in 1980. In the course of that disaster, he dumped five balls in Rae's Creek.

---

In the history of the Masters, each of the par-fives has been double-eagled exactly once.

Jordan Spieth holds the record for most birdies in a single tournament (28). Jack Nicklaus holds the record for most career birdies at the Masters, with 506.

---

Only six players have birdied the 72nd hole to win the Masters: Art Wall, Arnold Palmer, Gary Player, Sandy Lyle, Mark O'Meara and Phil Mickelson.

---

"If your ball is lodged in an orange, you cannot take relief without penalty." — USGA decision 23/10.

---

"If your ball comes to rest next to a cactus, you may wrap an arm or leg in a towel to protect yourself from the needles when you play your shot. But you can't cover the cactus with a towel." — USGA decision 1-2/10.

If a shot ends up in the clubhouse, and the clubhouse is not out-of-bounds, you can open a door or window and play the next shot without penalty.

Craig Stadler saved himself a laundry bill but costed himself $37,000 in prize money when he hit an illegal shot underneath a pine tree in a muddy lie in which he knelt down. Due to this going down as an incorrect scorecard he was disqualified.

At the 1979 U.S. Open Lon Hinkle found a significant shortcut on the 8th hole by using the fairway for the 17th hole. The officials then planted a 24-foot Black Hills spruce to block future shots.

The game of golf has been governed by 34 rules of play supported by 1,100 decision based on actual golf situations.

A "condor" is a term given to a hole-in-one on a par 5. It is almost as rare as two hole-in-ones in a single game of golf.

Almost 80% of golfers will never have a handicap under 18.

Alan Bartlett Shepard Jr. used a 6-iron to play golf on the moon.

The longest putt was a mind-blowing 375 feet.

# Jack Nicklaus had a 24 years difference between his first and last Major win

The very first nationally-televised golf tournament, the 1953 World Championship of Golf, featured an incredible finish from Lew Worsham.

Alice Miller presently holds the LPGA Tour's record for fastest round, completing 18 holes in one hour, 26 minutes, and 44 seconds.

Northern Canadian territory Nunavut's annual Toonik Tyme Festival includes a nine-hole golf tournament. With temperatures well below freezing, golfers play on a sheet of ice, using fluorescent balls, in fear of losing them in the snow.

The first golf course in China opened in 1984, but by the end of 2009, there were roughly 600 in the country.

The majority of professional golfers work as club or teaching professionals and only compete in local competitions.

PGA Tour events have a first prize of at least 800,000 USD.

Senior major championships have competitors that are aged 50 and over.

England has 2270 Golf Courses which is the 4th most of any country behind Canada, Japan and USA.

Rory McIlory spent 100 weeks as the worlds number one ranked golfer.

There are 31 distinct member classifications for professionals with A-1 being the highest class.

The very central part of the ball is known as the 'sweet spot'.

Augusta National looks almost nothing like it originally did when it was first opened. It took 15 architects to make changes to the course since 1935.

In 1983, Harukanaru Augusta was the first 8-bit video game to feature Augusta National.

Gary Player is the only Masters Winner to not have his Jacket locked up at Augusta. He was able to keep it by "forgetting" to bring it back after he won the 61' tournament.

The colour of the famous jacket has changed over the years from forest green to hunter green. Due to the change in manufacturers and tailors the green colour of the jacket has many different hues.

Disqualification can result from cheating, signing for a lower score, or failing to adhere to one or more rules that lead to improper play.

---

Many golfers wear golf shoes with metal or plastic spikes designed to increase traction, thus allowing for longer and more accurate shots.

---

As the game of golf has evolved, there have been many different putting techniques and grips that have been devised to give golfers the best chance to make putts.

---

The two basic forms of golf are known as stroke play and match play.

The only non American to win a major in 2019 was Shane Lowry.

---

The Players Championship has a $12,500,000 Prize Pool.

---

The 11th, 12th and 13th holes at Augusta National are famously known as Amen Corner.

---

Royal St George's Golf Club is based in an English town called Sandwich.

There were two unofficial matches between professionals from Great Britain and the United States before the birth of The Ryder Cup in 1927, both won by the British.

---

Nowadays the Ryder Cup matches pit the United States against all of Europe, but that was not always the case. From 1927 to 1979 the International opponents to the USA were only made up of players from Great Britain.

---

Europe had to wait a staggering 28 years to win the cup from the USA in 1985.

---

Sir Nick Faldo holds the record for the most Ryder Cup points with an astonishing 25.

On Tuesday night of the masters tournament week, the last year's winner gets to host a Champions Dinner. That winner chooses what will be on the menu for all past winners of the tournament.

---

A clubface that is one degree off at impact will cause your ball to fly two and a half yards off line on a shot that carries 100 yards.

---

An average golfer swinging a 56 degree wedge at 70mph will generate a spin rate at impact of approximately 10, 200rpm.

---

The Ryder Cup is named after the English businessman Samuel Ryder who donated the trophy.

Development of new golf courses is banned in China.

25K Golf balls are hit into the water at the 17th hole of the Stadium Course at Sawgrass each year.

You're more likely to get hit by lightning than make two holes-in-ones.

Each golf ball manufacturer creates different numbers of dimples on their golf balls.

There was a 10-year gap between 1937 to 1947 due to World War 2.

The European and US teams have 12 players each chosen by a captain.

Captains don't play in the Ryder Cup. The last playing captain for the Europe was Dai Rees in 1961, and the last for the USA was Arnold Palmer in 1963, from then to now the captains just pick the pairings and watch the golf.

Match play is a scoring system for golf in which a player, or team, earns a point for each hole in which they have bested their opponents; as opposed to stroke play, in which the total number of strokes is counted over one or more rounds of 18 holes. Match play encourages more aggressive play as players are looking to win the hole outright.

The Ryder Cup has ended in a draw two times, both in 1969 and then 20 years later in 1989. On a tie, the team that previously won retains the cup.

The largest margin of victory in the British Open was 13 strokes by Old Tom Morris in 1862.

The oldest competitor in the British open was Gene Sarazen, who was aged 74 years, 4 months, 9 days in 1976.

The only time the British Open was only played outside England and Scotland was 1951, at Royal Portrush Golf Club, County Antrim, Northern Ireland. The tournament returned to here in 2019.

In 2004, at the age of 39, Todd Hamilton became the oldest golfer to win PGA Tour Rookie of the Year.

In 1967, Arnold Palmer became the first golfer to reach one million dollars in career earnings on the PGA Tour.

Jack Nicklaus, considered by many critics to be the greatest golfer of all time, was known as "The Golden Bear"

British player Luke Donald topped the European Tour and the PGA Tour money lists in 2011.

Arnold Palmer was nicknamed 'The King'.

Following Europe's historic comeback victory at the 2012 event at Medinah Golf Course, the victory was nicknamed the 'Miracle at Medinah'.

The Ryder Cup is played in match play format.

Yang Yong-eun won the 91st PGA championship in 2009 and became the first Asian major winner in men's golf.

There are approximately 250 golf courses in Thailand. Thousands of tourists fly into Thailand every year just for the golfing opportunities offered in the country.

# The Ryder cup consists of 12 players on each team.

Jack Nicklaus won his first national golf title at aged 17.

Sam Snead finished 26 times in the top 25 at the Masters in Augusta.

The 'club with a metal head' is a nickname given to the iron club.

---

The Gutta golf ball replaced the Featherie ball.

---

The Payne Stewart award is given to a player whose values align with the character, charity and sportsmanship showed.

---

Most drivers are at least 45 inches long and are the longest club used.

The Masters is the only major that Rory McIlroy is yet to claim.

The maximum mass a golf ball can weigh is 1.62oz.

Tiger Woods has won the Masters 5 times.

Tony Jacklin was the first golfer to make a hole-in-one on television.

James the 2nd was the Scottish King to ban golf in 1457.

Tiger Wood's first name is actually Eldrick.

The trophy given to the winner of the Open Championship is known as The Claret Jug.

The Masters is the first of the four major tournaments to be held each year.

Jim Furyk recorded the lowest score of 58 in the final round of the 2016 Travelers Championship.

Angel Cabrera was the first South American to win the U.S. Open in 2007.

Tiger Woods is the only golfer to hold all 4 modern Major titles at the same time. he won the U.S. Open, Open Championship, and PGA Championship in 2000 and the 2001 Masters.

Sandy Lyle was the first British golfer to win the Masters in 1988.

There was an American boom in golf after American amateur Francis Ouimet won the U.S. Open in 1913 at 20 years old.

---

Phil Mickelson's first PGA Tour Victory occurred in 1991 at the Northern Telecom Open.

---

Mulligan is the term used when you hit a ball and decide to shoot the same shot again in amateur golf rounds.

---

The Memorial Tournament was founded in 1976, where Roger Maltbie defeated Hale Irwin on a sudden death playoff.

You have now come to the end of the book. I really hope you have enjoyed the book and have learned lots of awesome facts about the great sport of golf to impress your friends and family.

As a small independent publisher, positive reviews left on our books go a long way to attracting new readers who share your passion for the sport.

If you are able to take some spare time out of your day to leave a review it would be greatly appreciated.

If you spot any issues you would like to raise please **do email me before leaving a negative review** with any comments you may have.

I will be more than happy to liaise with you and can offer refunds or updated copies if you are unhappy with your purchase.

**TheUtopiaPress@gmail.com**

Printed in Great Britain
by Amazon

16414228R00032